For Dave and Lindsay
Mr and Mrs Games

First published in 2013 in Great Britain by
Barrington Stoke Ltd
18 Walker Street, Edinburgh, EH3 7LP

www.barringtonstoke.co.uk

ISBN: 978-1-78112-188-7

Printed in China by Leo

you killed me!

Keith Gray

Barrington Stoke

Contents

Chapter 1
Dead Man

It was three in the morning and the man at the end of the bed had a hole in his head. One of his eyes was gone. The hole was the size of a golf ball and ragged and messy. Most of the back of his head wasn't there any more.

I'd been dreaming. When I woke up and saw the man I really, really hoped I still was dreaming.

I felt instant panic. It was like icy electricity had shocked my body and I tried to shout but no sound came out. I kicked and bucked and scrambled back on my bed. But the wall was behind me. There was nowhere to go.

The man stepped closer. I couldn't tell how old he was. Maybe as old as my dad. He was dressed in blue workman's overalls that were spattered with white paint. His hair was black and slicked back in the kind of style Elvis had. He had a cricket bat in his hand. He leaned over me and I could see the full horror of his face. There was a dribble of red down his cheek as if he'd been crying blood.

"Are you Toby Link?" he asked me.

I couldn't speak. I couldn't breathe.

He leaned closer and I thought he was going to hit me with the cricket bat. I held my hands up to protect my head.

"You are Toby Link," he said. "I know that's who you are."

My heart was beating so fast I was scared it might explode inside me.

The man pointed at the hole where his eye used to be. "You did this," he said. "You killed me!"

I shook my head. I tried to say, 'No.'

"Look at it," the man said. He stuck a finger into the hole in his face. "A bullet. Bang. Right through my head. Because of you."

I closed my eyes and shook my head. Was this man a ghost? A zombie? Maybe it was only a dream?

"You're not real," I said out loud. I felt like I had wet cement in my mouth. I couldn't seem to swallow. "You're not a real ghost. You're a dream."

The ghost laughed at me. He rubbed his finger around inside the bullet hole where his eye had been, then used it to smear a sticky streak of red down my cheek.

"I'm real," he said. "I'm very real."

And I didn't know whether I was going to puke or scream.

Chapter 2
The Cricket Bat

"If I wanted to hurt you," the ghost said, "I could have done it while you were asleep. You'd never even have woken up. You'd be dead already. Just like me."

I swallowed again and again, trying to keep my fear down and under control.

I love *Batman*, *Hellboy*, *Battlestar Galactica*, *The Walking Dead*. I love all the stuff my older brother, Josh, says is for 'freaks and weirdoes'. I'm a geek. I have the movie posters on my walls, and comics in piles on the floor. The ghost looked like he might have crawled right out from the pages of my horror comics.

My mum says I should read 'nice' books, but I don't think there's any such thing. She probably means books for 5-year-olds about rabbits that talk and go shopping for hats.

My dad says I should grow up and read books about 'real things' and 'real people'. But I reckoned even my dad would have to admit the ghost was real. Totally, no question, 100% real.

I just wished he wasn't.

When the ghost came close to me I could feel how cold he was. It was a warm June night outside, yet here in my small bedroom the ghost was like a walking winter mist. And he smelled dead too. On Sundays I sometimes help my parents cook dinner. The ghost smelled like a lump of raw beef before you put it in the oven. It made me wonder if I'd ever want to eat Sunday dinner again.

"Do you believe I won't hurt you?" the ghost asked. "I won't. Not unless I have to."

"What do you want?" I asked back. I was buying time while I looked for a way to escape.

ould I push past him and make it to my
edroom door before he stopped me?

The thought of pushing him, touching him,
made me shudder.

"I want you to help me," he said. "You *are*
going to help me. You have to."

I wondered if I could shout for help. But even
if my parents heard me, and even if they believed
me, I guessed it would take them too long to run
from their room to mine. The ghost would have
plenty of time to swing that cricket bat in his
hand, and crack it against my skull.

And my brother Josh wouldn't believe me
even if I had photos to prove a million ghosts had
been having a party in my room.

"You can undo it," the ghost said.

"Undo what?" I asked.

"You killed me," the ghost said. He ran a
hand through his hair. "So you can undo it."

"No." I shook my head because this was all so
stupid. "I didn't kill you. I couldn't have. I don't
even know who you are."

The ghost frowned at me with his gaping, bloody face. "Look, kid," he said. "Toby. I'm trying to be nice now, aren't I? And I need you to understand what's at stake here. And that's me. My name's Len Grimsby. You're Toby Link. And you did this. Do you see it? I wouldn't be here if it hadn't been for you. This bullet hole is all because of you."

"But I don't have a gun," I said. I wanted him to go, to leave me alone. Maybe if I got him to understand it wasn't me who'd killed him, he'd just ... disappear.

I wished he'd appeared in my brother's bedroom. Josh was 16 and he was braver than me, cleverer than me, harder than me. Josh would know what to do.

"How could I have shot you?" I asked. "I've never even seen a gun, not in real life."

"You didn't shoot me," the ghost of Len Grimsby said. "You killed me with this." He held up the cricket bat.

"But – " I said. "But – " My head was a mad mess of fear and confusion.

The ghost held out the cricket bat for me to see. "Look at it? See? It's not just any cricket bat, is it?"

I peered at it in the darkness. I saw the worn and tatty green tape round the handle, and the letters 'TL' scratched into the wood.

"It's mine," I said, amazed. This was getting weirder and weirder and weirder. "But I threw it ..."

"You threw it away," the ghost finished for me. "Right. And it killed me."

"But – " was all I could say.

"But nothing," the ghost said.

"How did you get it?" I asked.

"I went back for it when I worked out I was dead." The ghost said this like it was the most obvious answer in the world.

I wish I could explain what was going on inside my head. There were too many thoughts fizzing around in there for me to think straight.

"OK, grab the bat," the ghost said, holding the cricket bat out to me. "Here, grab hold. Then maybe I can get you to believe me."

I didn't want to grab anything.

"If you don't grab it," the ghost said. "I might just have to hit you with it." He waited. "So?"

I reached out my hand.

Chapter 3
Yesterday Me

As soon as I touched the cricket bat it was as if I'd been dropped into an icy swimming pool of pure white light. It was a shock. I screwed up my eyes and sucked in my breath at the shocking cold of that white light.

When I opened my eyes again I wasn't in my bed any more, I was outside in the warm sunshine. The ghost stood next to me. He still had one end of the cricket bat and I had the other.

"Right, listen," the ghost said. "This bit might get confusing, but you're not daft, are you? I reckon you'll suss it out."

I wondered if anything could be more confusing than what had already happened.

"Where am I?" I asked, looking around. It was bright and sunny. There was grass and trees. It seemed to be some kind of park.

The ghost leaned close to me, loomed over me. "I said 'listen'. I never said 'talk'."

"But ..."

"Shut up with your 'buts'. Don't let go of the cricket bat, and listen. We are now in *yesterday morning*." He said it very slowly. "This is a replay of what happened."

"Yesterday morning?"

The ghost glared at me with his one good eye. "I'm getting fed up of repeating myself," he said. "We've gone back in time and this is now yesterday morning. This is the time when you were on the way to school."

"How can ...?" It was like trying to solve a million Maths problems all at once. "But ..."

"Keep hold of the cricket bat!" the ghost shouted. "If you let go we'll be right back in your bedroom, and we'll have to start all over again. I might not have time for that."

I didn't like standing so close to the ghost. Even though the sun was warm, he oozed cold like when you leave a fridge door open. But I took hold of the bat with both hands.

The ghost nodded. "Good. Right." He looked around. "See, over there. There you are."

And when I looked the way he pointed I saw the most amazing thing I'd ever seen. I saw *me*. Walking along, with my schoolbag on my back, carrying my cricket bat. And it was like watching the most amazing movie ever. It was like watching a movie in *4D*, if such a thing was even possible.

At last I understood where we were. "This is Camber Park," I said. "I'm walking to school. Yesterday morning."

"I don't want you to talk," the ghost told me. "Every time you open your mouth you just end up getting on my nerves. So shut up and watch what happens, OK?"

I did as I was told. The ghost and I moved closer to the other me who was walking along the path at the side of the park, yesterday morning, carrying my cricket bat.

I watched Yesterday Me walk along. I saw Yesterday Me looked totally fed-up. 100% miserable. And I remembered what Yesterday Me had been thinking back then. Yesterday Me had been thinking how much I hated cricket. There were patches of bright daffodils beside the path and Yesterday Me swung the bat at them, hitting the yellow flower heads for six.

My brother Josh loved cricket and was on the school team. But I hated cricket and was rubbish at it and only pretended to like it because Josh did. He said it was his favourite thing in the whole world ever. Mum and Dad were always proud of him when he won cricket matches and I wanted them to be proud of me as well. Yesterday Me was late for school but Yesterday Me didn't care because it was cricket practice at lunchtime and I knew I'd never be as good at it as Josh. Yesterday Me would be very happy never to have to do cricket practice ever again.

The footpath wandered between some trees and Yesterday Me swung the cricket bat at one of the trunks. Yesterday Me didn't swing it too hard but it made a loud thunk when it hit the tree.

And then Yesterday Me swung it harder, thunking it louder. Yesterday Me was wondering if it was possible to break the bat. Because how could you do cricket practice without a cricket bat? And then Yesterday Me began to wonder if there was a way just to *lose* the bat ...

A tall wooden fence runs all along the edge of the park, with the busy Camber Road on the other side. The fence used to be green, but it's been covered in graffiti and repainted so often it's all patches of different shades and colours. Yesterday Me turned and looked at the fence. Yesterday Me swung the cricket bat back and forth, thinking, wondering how tall the fence was. Then Yesterday Me swung the bat hard and high, and with a grunt threw it right over the top of the fence and out of sight.

Yesterday Me didn't hang around to see what happened next but ran off without a single glance back.

I stood with the ghost and watched Yesterday Me run, my school bag bouncing on my back. I remembered doing it, just as I had just seen it happen.

"See what you did?" the ghost asked me. "Yesterday morning, you threw your cricket bat away over the fence."

"But I went straight to school," I said. "I never saw the bat again, not until you ... not until now. I still don't understand how you think I killed you."

"It's what happened to the bat next," the ghost said. "We've got to follow that bat."

Chapter 4
Chain Reaction

Camber Road is always busy. The traffic rushes to and from the town centre. Cars, taxis, buses and delivery trucks. Camber Park runs along one side of the road, hidden for the most part behind the high wooden fence.

On the other side of the road from the park is a row of shops. There's a Chinese Takeaway called 'Dragon Bridge'. Its sign is all red and gold, written in that fantastic writing I wish I knew how to do. Next door there's a second-hand bookshop called 'Camber Reads', which is a great shop because it also sells old comics. Then there's the hairdresser's called 'Mary Artus', that my mum says is too expensive. It has a neon pink sign and the front is a huge window so you can see posh women having haircuts. The last shop in the row is the post office, with an old-fashioned, red post box right outside. The shops and the park mean that the pavements on either side of Camber Road are always as busy with people as the road is with traffic.

With another splash of cold, white light the ghost and I were suddenly standing on the pavement next to the Camber Park fence. I was so surprised I almost let go of the cricket bat.

"Don't," the ghost warned.

So I held on as tight as I could.

I was amazed that no one on the pavement seemed to see us. We had popped up like a pair of magic jack-in-the-boxes but no one noticed. No one looked twice at me in my pyjamas or the ghost with his Elvis hairdo and a hole in his head. I guessed this must be because it was all kind of a replay that the ghost and I were watching. We weren't really there.

There was a dad walking along with his young daughter and a tiny dog. The little girl could only have been about three or four and she toddled along holding onto her dad with one hand and the dog's lead with the other. She looked all happy and smiley with her dad and dog on a sunny day. I was glad she couldn't see the ghost of Len Grimsby's terrible face.

A lad on his bike was charging down the pavement the opposite way. I knew him from school. He was a 6th-former called Martin Cooper. He had long hair and was wearing a T-shirt with some heavy metal band or other on the front. He had his head down and his long hair hung in front of his face. I could see the wires from iPod headphones trailing out from his ears. He was pedaling fast and I wondered if he was late for school. Even so, he should have been on the road, not the pavement.

"Watch out!" I shouted at the dad. I thought Martin was going to hit him or his daughter.

But of course none of them could hear me.

And then the ghost said, "Here it comes." He pointed up at the sky.

I saw the cricket bat Yesterday Me had thrown away come flying over from the park on the other side of the fence. Martin didn't see it, not with all that hair hanging in front of his eyes. It seemed to fall out of the sky and smacked him right on top of his head. The noise it made was a heavy, hollow clunk.

Martin cried out in pain. He nearly went over the bike handlebars as he swayed and wobbled. Then he lost control of his bike. Luckily he missed the dad and the daughter and their dog. He somehow managed to stay the right way up on his bike even though his feet had come off the pedals and the handlebars had twisted in his grip. Unluckily he bounced off the pavement and shot out into the traffic rushing by on the road.

The dad swore in shock and tried to grab at Martin to stop him, but he missed. The daughter screamed and started to cry. Their little dog barked and barked.

There was a bellow of horns from the passing cars as Martin wobbled into the road. Breaks screeched. Martin was dazed, stunned. I saw a taxi speed towards him. I thought it was going to hit him. But it skidded and swerved at the very last second. It slammed up onto the opposite pavement. Now I thought it was going to hit the post box outside the post office. But it swerved again. And smashed through the front of the women's hairdresser.

The front window of 'Mary Artus' exploded. It was like a massive glass bomb had gone off around the taxi's front end. Posh women shrieked and shouted. They jumped out of their seats and dived for the back of the salon as the taxi crashed to a halt. The pink neon sign above the salon door swayed back, forwards, backwards, then dropped off and shattered to pieces on the taxi's roof.

Back in the middle of the road more car horns bellowed, more breaks squealed. Martin finally toppled off his bike into a heap of long hair, headphone wires and spinning bike wheels. He clutched at his head where the cricket bat had hit him. The traffic was jammed up in both directions. The dad was still swearing, his daughter was still crying and their little dog wouldn't stop barking. There was uproar and mayhem all over Camber Road. And it had all been my fault.

I said to the ghost, "Did I do that? When I threw the cricket bat over the fence yesterday morning, is this what happened ...?"

The ghost didn't answer.

I wanted to help Martin. I wanted to make sure no one in the hairdresser's was hurt and that the taxi driver was OK.

"Are you the taxi driver?" I asked the ghost.

"Of course I'm not," he told me.

I saw that the Yesterday Cricket Bat had landed half-in, half-out of the gutter. The little dog went to sniff it, but the dad yanked on the leash as he ran into the road to help Martin. So I bent down to pick it up.

But the ghost said, "Leave it. We're not even close to finished yet.

Chapter 5

Cancelled

With that same weird splash of cold white light, the ghost of Len Grimsby and I were in the back of a car. It was a big car and the wide back seat was pale, shiny leather. My mum would call it *lush*. There was plenty of room for me and the ghost to hold the cricket bat between us.

The car was filled with classical music and perfume. I could only see the back of the driver's head because I was right behind her seat. She had curly silver hair like my gran but she was wearing a purple velvet coat with a fur collar. My gran never wore anything that wasn't grey or brown. But the lady driver spoke to herself just like my gran did.

"What *is* happening here?" she said to herself, as she slowed the car down. And then she said it again, in case she hadn't heard herself the first time. Her voice was as purple and velvety as her coat. I thought people only talked as posh as that on TV.

She couldn't see either me or the ghost, just like the people on Camber Road hadn't been able to see us. She had no idea we'd popped up on the back seat. When she looked in her rear-view mirror, she stared right through us.

"Is this still a replay of yesterday morning?" I asked the ghost, who nodded.

I was confused about why we were here. But I'd been either scared or confused the whole time since the ghost had shown up, and I was kind of getting used to it. So I just stayed quiet and waited to see what was going to happen next.

I noticed that the ghost squirmed on the seat next to me like he was nervous. It made me wonder if we were getting closer to the time when he'd died and if I was going to see it happen, right in front of my eyes. I didn't know if it was something I'd want to watch.

The old lady driver must have been a bit deaf or mad because she asked herself yet again, "What is happening here?" Maybe it was because the music was so loud.

She brought the car to a stop and pulled on the handbrake.

"Well," she said. "I have just no idea what's happening here."

I looked out the car's back window and saw we were in a traffic jam. It didn't take a Brain of Britain to realise it was the same traffic jam as the one on Camber Road. The traffic jam I'd caused when I threw my cricket bat over the fence from the park ... And hit Martin from the 6th form on the head ... And made him swerve his bike into the road in front of the taxi ... And made the taxi skid and crash into the hairdresser's window ...

"How annoying," the lady driver said. She tapped her fingers on the steering wheel with a sound like a ticking clock. The colour on her nails matched her coat and her voice. She turned in her seat and twisted her neck to look at the

Linwood Library
15 Bridge Street, Linwood, PA3 3DB, TEL:
0300 300 1188

Customer ID: *****7103

Items that you have checked out

Title: The first hunter
ID: 240958321
Due: 17 August 2023

Title: You killed me!
ID: 184175621
Due: 17 August 2023

Total items: 2
Checked out: 3
Overdue: 0
Hold requests: 0
Ready for collection: 0
20/07/2023 12:03

Thank you for using the bibliotheca SelfCheck
System.

other cars that were stuck in the jam. "Well, well, well," she said, and tapped the wheel faster.

She checked her watch. She told herself it was annoying again. She told herself it was very annoying indeed. She tapped the steering wheel. And checked her watch again. Then she reached for her handbag on the passenger seat. It was as big as a pillow and she had to rummage inside for what seemed like ages before she pulled out her mobile phone. She typed a number into it and turned down the car's radio, reducing the violins and trumpets to a whisper.

"Hello," she said into her phone. "Yes, hello? Is that the hair salon? Good. Hello. This is Mrs Harrow. Yes, that's right, Mrs Harrow. I have an appointment at 9 o'clock, but I'm afraid it seems I am going to be late. There's a terrible traffic jam, you see. And ..."

She waited while the person on the other end of the line spoke.

Then: "Oh my! A taxi, you say? Good Lord! Right through the window? Was the driver drunk?"

Mrs Harrow sat up in her seat and tried to stretch her neck far enough to be able to see along the road, hoping to see the accident.

"Well, no, of course," she said into the phone. "Yes, yes. I completely understand. I'm very glad no one was hurt. But what about my hair?"

She waited again.

"Yes. Yes, I will. But if you ask me, that driver should be arrested. When can I have another appointment? Hmm. That will have to do, I suppose. Thank you. Good bye."

And she ended the call.

"Well, well, well," she said to herself. "Now there's a thing."

She tapped her fingers against the wheel for a little while longer and craned her neck to see all around again.

"I may as well go home," she told herself. She shrugged. "Yes. That's what I may as well do."

She turned the volume back up on the radio and the sound of violins filled the car again. Then she turned the car around without looking, doing a U-turn in the middle of the road. She ignored the angry honking of horns from the other cars that had to shuffle and shunt to let her through. She just waved at them with her purple-painted fingers as she drove away.

The ghost squirmed more and more on the seat next to me. It was clear he was upset or nervous about something.

"This is going to be horrible," he said. "Who wants to have to watch themselves die?" He glared at me. "It's all your fault this, you know? All this trouble, and you've caused it."

I didn't know what to say to that, so I didn't say anything at all. I still didn't see how I could have killed him. I wondered if it was Mrs Harrow who'd shot him. Did she have a gun in her big handbag? At least, if this was a replay of what had happened yesterday, then Len Grimsby would see I hadn't been the one who'd pulled the trigger. And then maybe he'd leave me alone. And then I could forget this bizarre night had ever happened.

Chapter 6
Yesterday Len

Maybe it was all in my mind, but it felt like the ghost was getting colder. As I sat next to him on the back seat of Mrs Harrow's car, I began to shiver.

The ghost was also getting more and more upset. He couldn't sit still. He kept shaking his head. He was the one who was a ghost, but he looked more nervous than me.

We drove for about ten or fifteen minutes to the outskirts of town. I didn't know this area very well, but I had been there before because our school had once played a cricket match against an all-boys school that was somewhere close by. Our school had lost.

Even though I knew Mrs Harrow couldn't hear me because this was all just a weird replay, I still couldn't help whispering when I asked the ghost: "Do you know Mrs Harrow?"

He seemed annoyed that I'd asked. He pointed at the paint-spattered overalls he was wearing. "I'm a painter and decorator. I did her new dining room for her." Then he went silent again.

Mrs Harrow turned off the road and drove in some tall metal gates. She drove up a sweeping gravel drive that was lined with fir trees. The house at the top of the drive looked like it had been built at least a hundred years ago. It was three times as big as my house and covered in thick, green ivy. There were steps up to the front door. On both sides of the door there was a fat statue of a stone lion. They looked like they were guarding the door and I thought they were much cooler than my dad's garden gnomes.

Parked at the bottom of the steps was a van that should have been white, but was now dirty-grey. Its back doors were wide open. It had the words 'Len Grimsby, Painter and Decorator' in looping letters on the side.

I looked at the ghost sitting next to me. He loomed in closer to me with his terrible face and poked a finger at me.

"You," he said. "Stay quiet. Or else, OK? *Or. Else.*"

Mrs Harrow was talking to herself again. "Well now," she said. "This is unexpected. I wonder what this can be about."

She turned off the car's engine, and the radio with the loud classical music. Then she gathered up her huge handbag from the passenger seat and climbed out onto the drive. Her shoes crunched on the gravel as she hurried towards the steps up to her front door. The ghost and I climbed out of the car after her. We were still holding the cricket bat between us. Our feet made no sound on the gravel.

Mrs Harrow muttered to herself as she fished her house-keys out of her handbag. She was halfway up the steps to her door when it was shoved open from inside, banging back on its hinges. Mrs Harrow let out a gasp of surprise. A man walked out of the house carrying one of the biggest TVs I'd ever seen. He was wearing blue overalls and his black hair was slicked back like Elvis's. But there was no bullet hole through his head.

Not yet.

I looked at the ghost standing next to me. He ignored me. Refused to meet my eyes. Then I looked back at Yesterday Len Grimsby at the top of the stone steps, half-in and half-out of Mrs Harrow's front door. I saw that the pockets of his overalls were bulging. The right pocket had silver knives and forks sticking out of it. A gold necklace dangling from the left. The necklace was like a shiny snake with a fat red jewel for a head. It looked like it was trying to slither away down his leg.

Yesterday Len swore. Twice. Then he said, "Look, Mrs Harrow. I, er … I can explain."

Mrs Harrow had been shocked into silence. She stood as still as her lion statues. But then she pointed a finger at Yesterday Len. Her purple nail looked dark and deadly. "Thief!" she screamed. "Thief! Burglar!"

Standing beside me, the ghost of Len Grimsby hung his head and stared at his feet. He didn't want to watch. It was hard to read his face, with that horrible hole were his eye should be, but I think he was ashamed.

"Thief!" Mrs Harrow shouted. "Help! Police!"

Yesterday Len said, "Don't, Missus. Don't call the police. We'll put it all back, OK? I promise. Just don't call the police." His knees were bending under the weight of that massive TV. He was struggling to carry it.

But Mrs Harrow didn't listen. She was digging in her handbag, searching for her phone.

I heard the crunch of gravel behind me. I turned to see a man with glasses and a shaved head walk out from the back of Len Grimsby's van. He must have been inside the van all this time. He was wearing black jeans and a baggy red T-shirt.

"Who's that?" I asked the ghost.

"He's called Capper," the ghost said.

Capper was trying to creep up on Mrs Harrow but the gravel was very loud.

Mrs Harrow was louder still. "Thief!" she cried again. She didn't have a clue Capper was there. "Burglar!"

Yesterday Len saw Capper behind her. "No, Capper," he called out. "Capper, no! Don't do anything." He was still holding the massive TV but he tried to wave at the other man to stop.

By this time Capper had sneaked right up behind Mrs Harrow. I thought he was going to grab her. Or worse, hit her.

Mrs Harrow had at last found her phone inside her huge handbag. "Police," she shouted at it before she'd even dialled 999.

Capper was so close behind her that he could have plucked the hair on the back of her neck. It was then I saw the gun in his hand. A pistol.

"No, Capper. No!" Yesterday Len shouted. He tried to run down the steps, with the TV still in his arms.

Capper narrowed his eyes. There was sweat shining all over his bald head. He lifted the gun to aim at the back of Mrs Harrow's head and leaned in close to her.

"Put your phone away, you old bag," he whispered in her ear. "Put it away or I'll – "

Mrs Harrow screamed and spun on her heel. She screamed again when she saw Capper. She threw up her hands and staggered back. She was still holding her huge handbag and it swung up into the air. It hit the gun Capper was holding. It took him by surprise. The gun went BANG.

Yesterday Len had been halfway down the steps. He stumbled and tumbled back, throwing out his hands. He dropped the TV and it crashed and rolled down the rest of the steps in a mess of broken plastic and shattered glass. The knives and forks spilled out of his right pocket, the necklace fell out of the left one. It was all clatter and noise. And then, after only one or two seconds, it felt like the whole world had gone totally silent.

Capper threw the pistol away and ran. He skidded on the gravel and almost fell over in his hurry to get away, but he ran down the drive and out the tall gates.

Mrs Harrow had gone pale. Paler even than the ghost standing next to me. The hand holding her phone was shaking. "Ambulance," she said into the phone. "Ambulance. Hurry. Please hurry."

But it was already too late. Yesterday Len lay on his back, staring up at the sunny sky with only one eye.

"That's enough," the ghost of Len Grimsby said. "I don't want to see any more." He let go of the cricket bat we were holding.

And with another weird splash of cold white light, we were back in my bedroom.

Chapter 7

Still Dead

It wasn't yesterday any more. We were back in my bedroom and it was night. It was *now*.

I sat on the edge of the bed and tried to understand everything I had seen. My head felt like a balloon filled with too much water. I saw I was still holding the cricket bat and put it down on the bed next to me.

The ghost of Len Grimsby paced up and down beside my bed. "This is what you have to do," he said to me.

I didn't listen. "You're a burglar," I said. "You were robbing that old lady."

"That's not the point," he said. "Just listen. I'm dead, and I shouldn't be. I'm dead, because of you."

"I didn't shoot you," I said. "We just saw that other man do it. That other burglar. Capper. Who is he?"

"A mate from the pub," the ghost said. He shook his head. "At least, I thought he was a mate. I get him to help me out with the painting and decorating now and again – cash-in-hand stuff. When I was doing Mrs Harrow's dining room I heard her on the phone to the hairdresser, making an appointment to get her hair done. I told Capper about it, told him how rich she was. It was his idea to rob her when she was out. He reckoned she wouldn't miss her telly and the odd bit of jewellery. He said she'd just buy more. But she wasn't meant to come home early, was she? Her appointment wasn't meant to be cancelled. A taxi wasn't meant to smash through the hairdresser's window."

"Was Capper meant to have a gun?" I asked. "It was him who shot you. Not me."

The ghost scowled at me with his terrible face. "You listen to me, kid. You listen, OK?" He pointed at the cricket bat. "Capper shot me, but you killed me. If you hadn't thrown that bat away, none of this would have happened."

"If you weren't a burglar, you wouldn't be dead," I said. "If your horrible friend Capper hadn't had a gun – "

"I didn't know he had a gun," the ghost said. "How was I to know he had a gun?"

"Why didn't you show up in his bedroom tonight?" I asked. "You could have scared him like you've scared me. And forced him to change things. Not to bring his gun or something."

The ghost paced up and down some more. "OK, right, I'm sorry," he said at last. "Maybe I shouldn't have scared you. But I had to come here to you because you started it all."

I looked at the cricket bat next to me. "And what will happen if I don't change things. What happens if I don't undo it?"

"I stay dead," the ghost said. "Forever. This is probably the only second chance I'll get. So you will help me, won't you? You will undo it?"

"I don't know how," I said.

I could tell the ghost was stuck then. He didn't know whether to threaten me or try to be nice to me. "All you've got to do is pick up the cricket bat by yourself," he said. "And when you do, you'll go back to yesterday morning again. But you'll go back for real this time. You won't just be watching. You'll really *be* there. And then, back in yesterday, all you have to do is keep the bat. Don't throw it away. Keep it, and none of this will happen. I won't be dead."

He waited, watching me. I didn't know what to do or what to say. He was a burglar. And it wasn't me who'd shot him.

"Just take the cricket bat," he said. "Just pick it up, OK? Pick it up and go back and change things. Stop me from being dead."

But I didn't know if I wanted to change things. "If I don't throw the bat away, then none of the things you've shown me will happen," I said. "Mrs Harrow's appointment won't be cancelled. She'll go to the hairdresser's, and when she gets home you really will have robbed her. You'll still be a burglar."

The ghost towered over me. I could feel cold leaking out of him. His breath was arctic. "I don't want to be dead," he said. "You have to change what happened or – "

Just then my bedroom door was flung open, startling me, and the light went on. The sudden brightness made me shut my eyes.

My brother stood in the doorway in his pyjamas. Most days he spends at least an hour fiddling with his hair in the mirror because he reckons all the girls fancy him. I think it's all a waste of time because he still doesn't have a girlfriend.

Now it was the middle of the night and he was angry at being woken up. His hair just looked like a giant fur-ball had exploded on his head.

"Who're you talking to?" he asked.

I looked around my room, but the ghost of Len Grimsby had disappeared.

"No one," I said.

Josh came over to me and punched me hard on the arm. "Then shut up, you weirdo. Let us normal people get some sleep."

He punched me again. Then he walked out, slamming my door on the way back to his own room.

I waited but the ghost of Len Grimsby didn't reappear. I didn't touch the cricket bat. I wondered if I'd imagined everything that had happened. Or had it really been a dream? But deep down, I knew it wasn't. I knew it was real. I could still feel the icy chill where the ghost of Len Grimsby had stood.

I left my light on and crawled under my covers to get warm. I looked at the comic and movie posters I had on my walls. This stuff that was happening to me felt like it should just be a story. It was like some freaky fantasy that should happen to one of my favourite cartoon heroes, not to me.

I was tired but I couldn't sleep. I had so many thoughts splashing around inside my head. And I wanted to keep my eye on that cricket bat, as if it was a deadly snake that might suddenly bite me if I was stupid enough to look away.

It was a long night.

Chapter 8
That Morning

In the end, I stayed awake all night long. I was scared the ghost of Len Grimsby was going to come back and force me to pick up the cricket bat.

He didn't come back.

And I didn't touch the bat.

I knew it would be easy to save Len Grimsby's life. All I had to do was pick up that bat, go back to yesterday morning, and *not* throw it over Camber Park's fence. What could be simpler? If I *didn't* throw it away, I could change the course of history.

Martin Cooper would not get smacked on the head and ride his bike out into the road.

The taxi would not swerve to miss him and smash into the Mary Artus salon.

Mary Artus would not cancel Mrs Harrow's appointment.

Mrs Harrow would not get home early and catch Capper and Len Grimsby in the middle of robbing her.

Capper would not threaten Mrs Harrow with a gun, she would not hit him with her handbag, and the gun would never fire ...

In Geography at school we'd learned about earthquakes and tidal waves and hurricanes. And I'd learned a new word: *aftermath*. It meant what was left behind after the disaster had struck. All of the smashed cars and destroyed houses and dead people were the *aftermath*.

I couldn't help thinking of everything that happened after I'd thrown my cricket bat away as the *aftermath*.

I knew what had happened to Len Grimsby, but I also wanted to know what had happened to Martin Cooper. Had I killed him too? He had been half-dead when he fell off his bike in the middle of the road. And what about the taxi driver? And the hairdressers? I had to know.

I crawled out of bed at about 7 feeling shattered with thinking so much. My brother was already in the bathroom, fiddling with his hair in front of the mirror.

"What are you looking at, weirdo?" he asked. He scooped a shiny glob out of the pot of gel he had balanced on the edge of the sink and rubbed it through his hair.

I was too tired for any brotherly agro. I asked, "Do you know Martin Cooper? Is he in your year?"

"He's a heavy-metal head-banger with greasy hair," Josh told me. "He looks like a yeti and plays guitar in the world's worst band. He's a freak, just like you. The two of you should be best friends."

He thought he was being funny. I ignored the insult. "Was he at school yesterday?" I asked.

"No, he was in hospital or something. Lucky git. We had this rock-hard Maths exam. But don't worry – your brilliant brother did brilliantly. Because I'm brilliant."

While Josh stared at himself in the mirror I squeezed some toothpaste into his pot of hair gel. I wondered how long it would take him to notice. But didn't hang around long enough to find out. I went back to my bedroom to get dressed.

I didn't touch the cricket bat. And I didn't go to school either. I put on my uniform and took my school bag, but I didn't go anywhere near the school itself. I went to the hospital instead. I wanted to find out what had happened in my *aftermath*.

Chapter 9
The Aftermath

I had worried Martin would still be knocked out, in bed with big bandages round his head. Maybe tubes coming out of his nose too. Maybe even hooked up to one of those machines that goes 'blip' every now and again. I'd seen that kind of thing on TV shows about hospitals and my imagination was in over-drive.

But Martin wasn't even in a bed when I got to the hospital. He was outside in the sun, sitting on a bench near the main door. He was wearing jeans and a heavy metal t-shirt and listening to his iPod while he watched the nurses rush about.

And there was only one small, white bandage on his head. His long hair hid most of it.

I walked over to him. "Hi," I said. "Hi, Martin."

He pulled the ear-buds from his iPod out of his ears. I could hear tinny music leaking out of the ear-buds.

"Do I know you?" he asked.

"I've seen you at school," I said. "I heard you were in an accident."

"Yeah," he said. "It was very cool." He went to put his ear-buds back in.

I was shocked. "Cool? But didn't it hurt?"

"Oh yeah, yeah. It hammered, man. Totally hammered. You try getting hit on the head by a flying cricket bat. It hammers."

"So what was so cool about it?" I asked.

He grinned and leaned towards me, as if he was telling me a secret. "I was meant to have this Maths test, and I was late. I mean, I would've been done for being late anyway, but I hadn't even revised. I've already failed once before, and my mum said she was gonna make me change schools if I failed again. She says my mates have a bad effect on me or something. But no way do I want to go to another school, man. Me and my mates have got a band going. We're gonna be well famous." He grinned at me and pointed at the bandage on his head. "Now I don't have to do the exam until next week. I've been given time to recover, see? Loads of time to revise. So it's cool, yeah?"

I shrugged. "I suppose so."

He grinned even wider. "And listen to this, OK. My mum's on her way to pick me up now. I'm waiting for her. She feels well sorry for me, because she reckons I could've been killed and that, so she's gonna buy me a new guitar. She's gonna take me to the music shop today and let me pick any one I want. How cool is that? I'm telling you, whoever threw that cricket bat did me a serious favour, man. So it's all very, very cool, yeah?"

I wondered if I should tell him it was me who threw the bat. But I decided not to.

I turned away as he put his ear-buds back in and turned up his music even louder. I walked away thinking his aftermath wasn't the kind I'd been expecting.

I wanted to find out more, so I headed over to Camber Road to see what kind of a state the Mary Artus salon was in.

I saw the answer straight away. In between the post office and the second-hand bookshop was a huge brown sheet of plywood where the big glass window of Mary Artus used to be. I saw a little bit of shattered glass twinkling on the pavement in the morning sun, but most of it had been cleared up. At least there wasn't a taxi stuck half-in, half-out any more.

A notice stuck to the plywood said, 'Closed until further notice.' I tried to peer round the edge of the sheet of wood to see inside. I wanted to know how bad the damage was in there. A voice behind me made me jump.

"What do you want?"

It was a woman with dyed red hair, all dressed up in very trendy clothes. She looked about 30, but I reckoned she was trying to look 20. I thought she looked like one of those people who fail to get on *The X Factor*. She was wearing a name badge that said 'Carly'.

"Sorry," I said, as I stepped away. "I was just, er ..."

"Just being nosy?" she said. "Well, if you're looking for dead bodies you're in the wrong place. No one here got so much as a scratch. Can you imagine how lucky we were?"

"You work here?" I asked. "You were here when it happened?"

"Oh, yes, I was here. I'm Head Stylist," she said. "But today it looks like I'm Head Sweeper-Upper. Same as I was yesterday, after Mary's boyfriend parked his taxi right in the middle of my 9 o'clock cut and blow-dry."

"Mary's boyfriend?" I said. "Do you mean Mary Artus? The owner?"

The Head Stylist gave me a long, hard stare. "You're asking a lot of questions. Shouldn't you be in school?"

"I'm on my way to school now," I said, "but my mum asked me to find out when you were going to be open again. This is her favourite hairdresser. She always comes here." I was pleased with the lie, and with how fast I'd told it. I sneaked a look at the Head Stylist's name badge again. "My mum says Carly always cuts her hair the best."

The Head Stylist smiled at me. "Aren't you a cutie-pie? Well, tell your mum that what happened is the best gossip she'll have heard all week. No – the best gossip all year. It turns out the taxi driver was Mary's old boyfriend from school. Can you imagine? They were in love all that time ago when they were 16. But they lost touch when they left school, and they didn't even clap eyes on each other again for 25 years. Not until he crashed his taxi right through the salon's front window yesterday!"

"Wow," I said. And I meant it too.

"Exactly," Carly said. "That's just it, isn't it? *Wow*." She was loving telling me the story. "And the best part is, they've fallen in love all over again. Can you even begin to imagine it? He's not *my* type, of course. But each to their own, as they say. Mary's already talking about marrying him. It'll be her fourth wedding. And it would never have happened if he hadn't crashed his taxi. Imagine that!"

I promised I'd tell my mum 'the gossip' and thanked Carly as I walked away. I was surprised by everything that she and Martin had told me. In their own ways, they were both saying it was a good thing I threw the cricket bat away. I was keen to find out what Mrs Harrow would say.

It took me about half an hour to walk to Mrs Harrow's house. The tall metal gates were open and so I went in and walked up the long drive with my feet crunching on the gravel. I was trying not to think too much about what I'd seen happen here – the replay I'd been given of Len Grimsby's death. I wished I knew where his ghost was right now. I felt a sharp chill on the back of my neck and wondered if he was watching me.

I reckoned he wouldn't be happy that I hadn't picked up the cricket bat yet. It seemed to me that he was the only one who wanted things to change. Both Martin and Mary Artus had something good happen to them because I threw away the bat. As I walked up the drive to Mrs Harrow's house, I was pretty sure she would be happy with the way things had turned out too. She hadn't been robbed after all.

Mrs Harrow's car was parked on one side of her ivy-covered house. Len Grimsby's van was nowhere to be seen and I supposed the police had taken it away. Had they also taken Capper away? Had they even found him?

I hesitated before I walked up the stone steps to the wide front door of the house. It was hard to believe I'd seen someone get shot and die here. I didn't know if the dark spots on the stone were old dirt or brand-new blood. I was careful not to stand on the spot where I thought Len Grimsby had fallen.

The door had an old-fashioned metal knocker. I knocked twice.

There was no answer.

I knocked again.

Still no answer. But I thought I heard some one on the other side of the door, inside the house.

"Hello?" I called. "Hello? Mrs Harrow?"

"I don't want to talk to any more police or any more reporters," the old lady said from the other side of the door. "I've answered enough questions."

"I'm not a policeman or a reporter," I shouted through the door. I waited, but she didn't answer. I leaned closer to the door, trying to hear anything from inside. "Mrs Harrow? Are you still there?"

"Who are you, then?" she asked. "What do you want?"

"My name's Toby," I said. But then I stopped. What did I want? That was a good question. "I want to know what the right thing is to do," I told her. That was the truth.

There was a click from the lock. Then I heard the scrape of a bolt being pulled back and Mrs Harrow opened the door. She looked different to yesterday morning. She didn't look purple, posh or proud any more. She looked more like my gran, like an old lady stooped and bent with the weight of all her years.

She looked me up and down. "You're a schoolboy," she said. "What on earth are you doing knocking on my door?"

"Yesterday morning – " I started.

"I really do not want to talk about yesterday morning," she said. "Not to anyone. Goodbye."

She went to close her door again.

"Please, Mrs Harrow, I just need to know one thing," I said. "Are you glad it happened?"

I'd shocked her. The look on her face was as if I'd thrown icy water down her back. "Glad?" she asked. "Am I *glad*?"

I nodded quickly. "Yes," I said. "Glad. Or pleased? You know, because you didn't get robbed, did you? Not in the end. You must be happy you've still got your TV and your necklace and – "

"*Pleased?*" She screamed the word at me. "*Happy?*" She prodded me in the chest with a bony finger, so hard it hurt. "Someone died!" she shouted. "A man died right here at my house, and I must take part of the blame, and you ask me – " She stopped, and when she spoke again, her voice shook. "You stupid, stupid boy. He died right on these steps where you are standing and you ask if I'm pleased? You have the nerve to ask if I'm *happy*?"

"I'm sorry," I said, backing off down the steps. "I didn't mean … I didn't think. I'm sorry."

She followed me down the steps, prodding me in the chest all the way. "No, young man. No, you didn't think, did you? What do I care about televisions and jewellery when a man died? See this? This is his blood you're standing in. I've scrubbed and scrubbed these steps, but ..." She looked down and I saw that she had bright, sharp tears in her old eyes. "If I could give all of my silly jewels away just to stop him dying here on my steps, I would do it in an instant. Do you understand? In a split second. Just to stop him dying. I don't care who he was, he didn't deserve to die, and I know I didn't deserve to have it happen in front of me."

Her words were all anger and horror and sadness tangled up together. I had never felt so stupid or ashamed before. All I could do was keep saying I was sorry, really sorry, as I turned and ran away back down her long drive.

Chapter 10
Reset

"Why am I still dead?"

The ghost of Len Grimsby was waiting for me when I got home.

"What's going on?" he asked. He was like a freezing fog in my room, making everything ice cold. Maybe he was scared. Scared I was going to let him stay dead forever. "Why haven't you picked up the cricket bat?" he wanted to know, "I told you – "

I was still upset and angry with myself because of what had happened at Mrs Harrow's house. But I also needed more answers to all the questions tangled up in my head.

"Tell me again what happens," I said. "When I pick up my cricket bat, tell me exactly what happens."

"I told you everything last night," the ghost said. "Why don't you ever listen?"

"Tell me again!" I shouted.

He paced up and down. If he hadn't been a ghost his boots would have been loud on the floor.

"When you pick up the bat you go back to yesterday morning, and everything gets reset," he told me. "I won't be there because I'll be alive again. But you will be there, really there. Not just watching things happen like it's a fancy film. So you'll be able to change things."

"Reset?" I asked.

"That's what I said, isn't it? Everything that's happened since yesterday won't have happened any more. Everything resets to when you were walking to school, and then it starts again. I won't even know who you are, because we won't ever have met."

'Reset,' I thought.

It meant Martin Cooper would fail his Maths exam and his mum would force him to move schools. He would lose his friends and his band. It also meant Mary Artus and the taxi driver would not meet again. They might never fall in love again like they had done when they were 16.

But reset also meant Len Grimsby wouldn't get shot, wouldn't be dead. And Mrs Harrow might still have her TV and stuff stolen, but she would never have to scrub bloodstains off her steps.

If only there was a way to make everything good for everyone.

The ghost broke in on my thoughts. "Just remember not to let go of the bat, OK?" he warned me. "Not once you've picked it up again. If you drop it or let it go then you come back here again and nothing will ever get reset. Understand?"

"I think so," I said.

"So, come on. What are you waiting for? Pick up the bat. I deserve a second chance, don't I?

Everyone deserves a second chance. Just pick up the bat, kid. Please."

I knew the time had come to choose, one way or the other.

I reached out for the bat.

Chapter 11
Yesterday Again

Cold ...

Splashing ...

White light ...

... and I was standing on the path at Camber Park once more. And it was yesterday morning again. But this time I was on my own, like the ghost of Len Grimsby had said. This time it was all real.

I walked along the path between the trees, remembering the way I had walked when I'd done this first time around. I was trying to repeat everything I'd done just the same. I swung the cricket bat to knock the heads off the daffodils. But at the same time, an idea was growing in my mind. I had decided I wasn't going to throw my cricket bat away, but I was beginning to wonder if I could make things happen the way I wanted them to as well.

I ran a little way along the path to the exact place I thought I'd thrown the bat over the fence the first time around. But instead of throwing it I jumped up at the fence and climbed to the top. I sat with one leg dangling down onto the side with the park and the other leg dangling over onto Camber Road. I shuffled along the top of the fence until the leaves of a tree hid me from sight. I didn't want to be seen.

Camber Road was busy. As I looked across the road I could see the row of shops and the Mary Artus salon with its big glass front and pink sign. I could see half a dozen women inside and thought I saw Carly the Head Stylist, but it was a bit too far away for me to be sure.

I looked up and down the pavement on my side of the road and saw the dad with his young daughter and their dog. The little girl was smiling, happy to be dragged along by her even littler dog. Everything seemed just as it should be.

I looked along the pavement the other way and saw Martin on his bike. Head down, earplugs in, peddling fast. For him *not* to get into trouble for failing his Maths exam, for him *not* to get sent to another school by his mum, he needed to get smacked on the head with my cricket bat. But I needed the bat to save Len Grimsby's life.

I gripped the top of the fence between my knees to steady myself. Martin couldn't see me up there. He raced towards me on his bike. I clutched the cricket bat in both hands, waiting, waiting. I knew if I missed this could all go very, very wrong. Martin came closer, closer. At the exact second he raced by me, I swung the bat.

It thunked so hard against his head that I got shudders all up my arms.

Martin yowled.

It was such a relief I hadn't missed.

This was the point when Martin was meant to wobble out into the road, into the way of the taxi. When I looked I could see the taxi coming. It was almost here. But Martin didn't wobble into the road. I'd hit him harder than I thought. He fell off his bike right there and then. He tumbled into a tangled heap on the pavement in front of the dad and his daughter.

The dad looked up at me where I was hiding in the tree branches. He pointed an angry finger at me.

"You," he shouted. "That was you, wasn't it? What on earth are you playing at? Why did you hit him?"

I began to panic. Not because of the angry dad, but because I could see the taxi getting closer. It was only six or seven cars away down the road. If it didn't swerve and crash into the front of the hairdresser's, then the driver and Mary Artus would never meet again. But Martin was in a heap on the pavement, not in the middle of the road. There was only one thing I could do. I had to be the one to run out into the road.

I clambered down from the fence and was about to run but the dad grabbed my arm.

"You're not going anywhere," he said. "Look at what you've done. You could have killed this lad." He pointed at Martin who was rolling on the ground, clutching his head and moaning.

"I was trying to stop him from failing Maths," I shouted at the dad as I tried to tug my arm away. "Let me go! I've done him a favour." The taxi was only three cars away now. "Let me go."

But the dad held on tight. "I'm calling an ambulance and the police," he said.

"You don't understand," I said. The taxi was two cars away.

The little girl was crying because of the noise and shouting. The dog was barking and jumping up at me. I waved my cricket bat as I fought to get away from the dad and the dog jumped up at it like it was a big stick.

The taxi was only one car away. It was going to drive right on by. The driver would never meet Mary Artus again if I didn't do something fast.

I waved my cricket bat at the dog. "*Fetch!*" I shouted.

I remembered what the ghost had told me about never letting go of the bat and I only pretended to throw it out into the road. But the dog tried to chase it anyway. It jerked its lead out of the little girl's hand. She screamed. The

dad swore. And the dog jumped out into the
traffic.

For one single split-second I was scared
the taxi driver wouldn't see such a small dog ...
But then the taxi's horn blared and its tyres
screeched as it swerved. It bounced up onto the
other pavement, just missed the post box outside
the post office, and smashed, shattered and
crashed through the glass front of Mary Artus's
salon.

The dad let go of me as he rushed into the
road and snatched the little dog up into his arms.
The dog wagged its tail but the daughter was all
wet sobs and howling tears. Cars jammed up on
both sides of Camber Road, and more horns fired
off. People shouted and bellowed as they ran to
the salon to make sure no one was hurt. I could
hear shocked women screaming inside. The pink
sign fell down and exploded on the taxi's roof.
Martin was still rolling around, groaning and
clutching his head.

I had never been happier.

But I knew I couldn't hang around. In the
middle of all the fuss no one tried to stop me as
I turned away and started running. I had to get

to Mrs Harrow's house. I had to get there as fast as I could. I knew I didn't have long to get there before her appointment got cancelled and she went back home. If she beat me, she would find Len Grimsby and Capper robbing her ... Capper would get his gun ... and she would swing her handbag ...

Chapter 12
Never Again

My throat burned, my heart hammered and my legs were heavy wet mud by the time I reached Mrs Harrow's house. I'd run all the way and I was still scared I was too late.

I didn't have a plan, not a proper one. I knew I wanted to get there before Mrs Harrow. Maybe I could talk to Len Grimsby. Maybe I could get him and Capper to leave. I was scared of Capper, but I thought I might be able to make Len see sense.

I wanted to rest and catch my breath but I didn't dare stop. I ran in Mrs Harrow's tall metal gates. I ran up the drive. My feet crunch, crunch, crunched on the gravel.

And I was too late. Mrs Harrow's car was already there. The old lady had beaten me home.

As I ran towards the house, I could see Len Grimsby at the top of her steps with that massive TV, his pockets full of silver cutlery and other stolen stuff. As I got closer I could hear Mrs Harrow calling him a thief. I was still too far away when Capper climbed out of the back of Len Grimsby's dirty white van and sneaked up behind the old lady.

I tried to shout but my breath had all gone. My warning came out as a hoarse whisper that only I could hear.

And I couldn't run any more. I felt like I didn't have a single drop of strength left in me. But I kept going. My feet kept crunch, crunch, crunching on the gravel. I had to stop Capper. I had to save Len. I didn't want Mrs Harrow to have to scrub his blood off her steps.

"No," I tried to shout, between panting breaths. "Stop. No. Please."

Nobody heard me.

Mrs Harrow took her phone out of her handbag. She shouted, "Police!" even before she dialled. Capper was only a few steps behind her. But I was getting closer, too. I ran round the side of Len Grimsby's van.

Capper was so close behind the old lady that he could have plucked the hair on the back of her neck. It was then I saw the gun in his hand. A pistol.

"No, Capper. No!" Len Grimsby shouted. He tried to run down the steps, with the TV still in his arms.

Capper narrowed his eyes. There was sweat shining all over his bald head. He lifted the gun to aim at the back of Mrs Harrow's head and leaned in close to her.

I was still running. I was still getting closer.

"Put your phone away, you old bag," Capper whispered in Mrs Harrow's ear. "Put it away or I'll – "

Mrs Harrow screamed and spun on her heel. She screamed again when she saw Capper. She threw up her hands and staggered back. She was still holding her huge handbag and it swung up into the air. It hit the gun Capper was holding. It took him by surprise. The gun went BANG.

And I jumped. I'd made it to the steps and I found my very last drop of strength and sprang forward. I dived in front of Len, with the cricket bat held in my stretched-out hand.

There was an instant burst of pain along my arm. The cricket bat tried to jump out of my hand but I held on tight. I held on tighter than I'd ever held onto anything before. And I fell full length onto the stone steps in front of Len Grimsby.

I heard him swear. He put the TV down and crouched over me. "Who the bloody hell are you?" he asked. "Are you OK?"

"You're alive!" I panted. "You're still alive."

Mrs Harrow was also standing over me. "Oh my goodness. Oh my, my, my. Who on earth ...? How on earth ...?" She looked at Len Grimsby. "This boy just saved your life."

Len Grimsby was stunned into silence.

He went to take the cricket bat off me but I wouldn't let him. The bullet from Capper's gun was sunk in the wood. The pain I'd felt in my arm had been the jolt of the bullet's impact.

"You saved my life," Len Grimsby said. And he said it like he might have said, "I've just seen a unicorn fly past in a spaceship." Like it was impossible to believe.

"You told me to," I tried to explain. "It was you who told me to stop you being dead."

But Len Grimsby didn't know what I was talking about. Of course he didn't, I told myself. Because everything had been reset.

Len helped me stand up. I rubbed my arm. It hurt but there was no blood. Neither mine nor Len Grimsby's. And I could see the bullet sunk bang in the centre of my cricket bat.

Len Grimsby pointed at Capper, who was trying to sneak away. "You nearly killed me," he said.

Capper seemed as shocked as everyone else. "I didn't mean to. It was an accident. I only wanted to scare her." He dropped the gun and turned to run.

I didn't really think about what I was doing. I threw my bat at him before he could run away.

I hurled it at him as hard as I could. It spun end-over-end and smacked him on the back of the head. He went down like a sack of spuds, face-first into the gravel. I'd knocked him out cold.

Only then did I worry about letting the cricket bat go. The ghost said nothing would ever be reset if I even so much as dropped it.

I stood on Mrs Harrow's steps and waited for something to happen now that I didn't have the bat any more. I waited for the cold splash of white light that would whisk me back to my bedroom again.

But nothing happened. Len Grimsby just said, "Good shot, kid." That was all.

And I realised that everything had already been reset when I had saved Len Grimsby's life. It couldn't be undone. Not now. Never again.

Chapter 13
Here and Now

Five minutes later, Mrs Harrow's gravel drive was crowded with two police cars and an ambulance. Len Grimsby looked glum as they cuffed his hands behind his back. Two officers led him down the steps and past his friend Capper, who was still knocked out and sprawled face-down on the gravel drive.

"Why did I ever listen to you?" Len had snarled at him. "I must be a moron to ever have listened to anything you said." He'd even aimed a kick at his former friend but the policemen pulled him away.

I saw all of this from behind a tree in Mrs Harrow's garden. I hadn't wanted to wait for the police and had sneaked away. I didn't know how on earth to explain what I was doing there saving lives and flinging cricket bats. I didn't think they'd believe me if I told them the truth and I was too tired to think up a clever lie.

Len Grimsby had seen me creep away. "Don't forget your cricket bat," he'd whispered. Then he'd watched me run off across the garden to hide behind the tree.

"Where's that brave young man gone?" Mrs Harrow had asked.

Len had only shrugged. As the policemen shoved him into the back of one of their cars he'd looked over at the tree where I was hidden. I was crouched down low so I was sure he couldn't see me. But it felt as if his eyes stared straight into mine.

"You saved me!" he'd shouted.

Then the police had bustled him into their car and slammed the door. They drove him away and I never saw him again.

Two medics rolled Capper's floppy, knocked-out body onto a stretcher and carried him into an ambulance.

"Good riddance to bad rubbish," Mrs Harrow shouted as they drove him away.

Then a policewoman took Mrs Harrow into the house. I could hear Mrs Harrow from my place behind the tree, telling the policewoman she wouldn't be answering any questions until she'd had a nice cup of tea, or maybe a small glass of brandy.

When they'd gone inside and no one was there to see, I climbed the garden wall and hurried away, taking my cricket bat with me.

Over the next couple of days I enjoyed reading the stories in the local newspaper, and even on Facebook, about a mystery boy who had saved an old lady from being burgled and a robber from being killed. It made me feel a bit like one of my favourite superheroes. I never told anybody it was me.

A few days later I checked up on Martin Cooper, and Mary Artus and the taxi driver.

Martin had still failed his Maths exam, so I guess there are some things that can't ever be changed. But he managed to talk his mum into letting him stay at our school. He changed the name of his heavy metal band to 'Real Men Don't Wear Helmets' and they've been allowed to play at this year's Prom. Martin will be playing his brand new guitar.

The Mary Artus salon has a brand new glass front and glowing pink neon sign. Mary is getting married to her long-lost taxi-driver boyfriend next month. Or so Carly the Head Stylist told me when I asked. Carly was very excited about it because now she's going to be Head Bridesmaid too.

I just wish my own aftermath could have been a bit more 'happy ever after'. But my brother Josh grassed me up for skipping school and cricket practice. My parents went mad. They grounded me for a whole month.

But I know I can never tell anybody the truth. The story is as amazing as anything in my favourite comics or movies. Who'd believe me? But I know it really happened. And I'll never forget Len Grimsby. Because I saved him!

Our books are tested
for children and young people by
children and young people.

Thanks to everyone who consulted on
a manuscript for their time and effort in
helping us to make our books better
for our readers.

*Also by **Keith Gray**...*

The Chain

Four people. Four stories. Four links in the chain.

Cal is sick of being the good guy. Joe's dad is a big-time loser. Ben has two girlfriends but only loves himself. Kate has to say the hardest goodbye of all.

One book, which will change their lives forever...

Ghosting

Nat's sister Sandy speaks to the dead. It's a gift.
And a good way to make a living.

Only thing is, it isn't true.

So imagine Nat and Sandy's surprise when the
dead start to speak back. But it seems the dead
are the least of their problems...

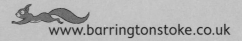
www.barringtonstoke.co.uk